OTHER GUIDED JOURNALS & DIARIES
by
KINYATTA E. GRAY

I Miss You...

Daily Writing Prompts for Reflection, Remembrance, and Spirit Renewal

My Crazy Teenage Life

The Ultimate Expression Diary for Venting, Self-Reflections and Self-Love

Fashionista's Travel Diary

A Guided Travel Diary for Travel Planning & Reflections

I Am A Man. I Have Feelings.

A Guided 90-Day Self-Reflections & Gratitude Journal for Men

I'm Doing Me

The Ultimate Breakup Diary for Venting, Reflection & Spirit Renewal

The Queen's Manifestation Journal

Daily Writing Prompt for Manifesting the Life You Want

While I'm Still Here

A Guided Expression Journal of Life, Love and Legacy for Those Preparing to Transition

Budget & Shop

A Monthly Personal Budget & Expense Tracker for Young Adults

amazon

How many times have you felt invisible in a room full of people? How many masks have you worn to hide your true identity? How many heterosexual relationships did you engage in pretending to be in love? What was your biggest fear when finally letting your family and friends know, you are a beautiful feminine lesbian?

Passing As "Straight": Beautiful Women Whose True Sexuality Went Undetected by a Judgmental Society, compiled by Author Kinyatta Gray, brings to life a book that takes a deep look into the individual, personal and complex stories of lesbians whose true sexuality went undetected to prevent labeling, judgment, or even death. Six courageous women will share real life situations where they had to make the dreadful decision of hiding their sexual identify to find acceptance, respect, and love from those who truly matter.

This book is not meant to define who's right or wrong, but rather examine this very real issue and the choices that lesbian women must make about love! Our intention is to provide a heartfelt resource for women who wake up daily having to navigate through a society pretending and hiding who they really are. You are not alone! We all have been there! But, as you read through these pages, you will find the comfort and strength to know exactly how to live unapologetically and uniquely who you are.

KINYATTA E. GRAY, CELEBRITY AUTHOR
INSTAGRAM: @KINYATTAGRAYTHEAUTHOR
WEBSITE: KINYATTAGRAY.COM

"THERE WILL NOT BE A MAGIC DAY WHEN WE WAKE UP AND IT'S NOW OKAY TO EXPRESS OURSELVES PUBLICLY. WE MAKE THAT DAY BY DOING THINGS PUBLICLY UNTIL IT'S SIMPLY THE WAY THINGS ARE."

~Tammy Baldwin

Today's Date:

I Feel:

☐ Supported
☐ Protected
☐ Happy
☐ Optimistic
☐ In Love
☐ Sad
☐ Angry
☐ Scared
☐ Unsupported
☐ Content

My Feelings and Thoughts

Today's Date:

<table>
<tr><td>

____

____

____

____

____

____

____

</td><td>

I Feel:

☐ Supported

☐ Protected

☐ Happy

☐ Optimistic

☐ In Love

☐ Sad

☐ Angry

☐ Scared

☐ Unsupported

☐ Content

</td></tr>
</table>

Today's Date:

I Feel:
☐ Supported
☐ Protected
☐ Happy
☐ Optimistic
☐ In Love
☐ Sad
☐ Angry
☐ Scared
☐ Unsupported
☐ Content

My Feelings and Thoughts

Today's Date:

I Feel:

- ☐ Supported
- ☐ Protected
- ☐ Happy
- ☐ Optimistic
- ☐ In Love
- ☐ Sad
- ☐ Angry
- ☐ Scared
- ☐ Unsupported
- ☐ Content

My Feelings and Thoughts

Today's Date:

I Feel:

- ☐ Supported
- ☐ Protected
- ☐ Happy
- ☐ Optimistic
- ☐ In Love
- ☐ Sad
- ☐ Angry
- ☐ Scared
- ☐ Unsupported
- ☐ Content

My Feelings and Thoughts

Today's Date:

I Feel:

- ☐ Supported
- ☐ Protected
- ☐ Happy
- ☐ Optimistic
- ☐ In Love
- ☐ Sad
- ☐ Angry
- ☐ Scared
- ☐ Unsupported
- ☐ Content

Today's Date:

____

____

____

____

____

____

____

I Feel:
☐ Supported
☐ Protected
☐ Happy
☐ Optimistic
☐ In Love
☐ Sad
☐ Angry
☐ Scared
☐ Unsupported
☐ Content

____

____

____

____

____

____

____

____

____

____

____

____

____

____

Today's Date:

I Feel:

☐ Supported
☐ Protected
☐ Happy
☐ Optimistic
☐ In Love
☐ Sad
☐ Angry
☐ Scared
☐ Unsupported
☐ Content

My Feelings and Thoughts

Today's Date:

I Feel:
☐ Supported
☐ Protected
☐ Happy
☐ Optimistic
☐ In Love
☐ Sad
☐ Angry
☐ Scared
☐ Unsupported
☐ Content

Today's Date:

I Feel:
- ☐ Supported
- ☐ Protected
- ☐ Happy
- ☐ Optimistic
- ☐ In Love
- ☐ Sad
- ☐ Angry
- ☐ Scared
- ☐ Unsupported
- ☐ Content

Today's Date:

I Feel:
☐ Supported
☐ Protected
☐ Happy
☐ Optimistic
☐ In Love
☐ Sad
☐ Angry
☐ Scared
☐ Unsupported
☐ Content

My Feelings and Thoughts

Today's Date:

I Feel:

- ☐ Supported
- ☐ Protected
- ☐ Happy
- ☐ Optimistic
- ☐ In Love
- ☐ Sad
- ☐ Angry
- ☐ Scared
- ☐ Unsupported
- ☐ Content

My Feelings and Thoughts

Today's Date:

I Feel:

- ☐ Supported
- ☐ Protected
- ☐ Happy
- ☐ Optimistic
- ☐ In Love
- ☐ Sad
- ☐ Angry
- ☐ Scared
- ☐ Unsupported
- ☐ Content

My Feelings and Thoughts

Today's Date:

I Feel:

- ☐ Supported
- ☐ Protected
- ☐ Happy
- ☐ Optimistic
- ☐ In Love
- ☐ Sad
- ☐ Angry
- ☐ Scared
- ☐ Unsupported
- ☐ Content

My Feelings and Thoughts

Today's Date:

<table><tr><td>

I Feel:

☐ Supported
☐ Protected
☐ Happy
☐ Optimistic
☐ In Love
☐ Sad
☐ Angry
☐ Scared
☐ Unsupported
☐ Content

</td></tr></table>

Today's Date:

I Feel:
☐ Supported
☐ Protected
☐ Happy
☐ Optimistic
☐ In Love
☐ Sad
☐ Angry
☐ Scared
☐ Unsupported
☐ Content

Today's Date:

I Feel:

- ☐ Supported
- ☐ Protected
- ☐ Happy
- ☐ Optimistic
- ☐ In Love
- ☐ Sad
- ☐ Angry
- ☐ Scared
- ☐ Unsupported
- ☐ Content

My Feelings and Thoughts

Today's Date:

I Feel:

☐ Supported
☐ Protected
☐ Happy
☐ Optimistic
☐ In Love
☐ Sad
☐ Angry
☐ Scared
☐ Unsupported
☐ Content

Today's Date:

I Feel:
☐ Supported
☐ Protected
☐ Happy
☐ Optimistic
☐ In Love
☐ Sad
☐ Angry
☐ Scared
☐ Unsupported
☐ Content

My Feelings and Thoughts

Today's Date:

I Feel:

- ☐ Supported
- ☐ Protected
- ☐ Happy
- ☐ Optimistic
- ☐ In Love
- ☐ Sad
- ☐ Angry
- ☐ Scared
- ☐ Unsupported
- ☐ Content

Today's Date:

I Feel:

☐ Supported
☐ Protected
☐ Happy
☐ Optimistic
☐ In Love
☐ Sad
☐ Angry
☐ Scared
☐ Unsupported
☐ Content

My Feelings and Thoughts

Today's Date:

I Feel:

- ☐ Supported
- ☐ Protected
- ☐ Happy
- ☐ Optimistic
- ☐ In Love
- ☐ Sad
- ☐ Angry
- ☐ Scared
- ☐ Unsupported
- ☐ Content

Today's Date:

I Feel:
☐ Supported
☐ Protected
☐ Happy
☐ Optimistic
☐ In Love
☐ Sad
☐ Angry
☐ Scared
☐ Unsupported
☐ Content

My Feelings and Thoughts

Today's Date:

I Feel:

- ☐ Supported
- ☐ Protected
- ☐ Happy
- ☐ Optimistic
- ☐ In Love
- ☐ Sad
- ☐ Angry
- ☐ Scared
- ☐ Unsupported
- ☐ Content

My Feelings and Thoughts

Today's Date:

I Feel:

☐ Supported
☐ Protected
☐ Happy
☐ Optimistic
☐ In Love
☐ Sad
☐ Angry
☐ Scared
☐ Unsupported
☐ Content

My Feelings and Thoughts

Today's Date:

I Feel:

☐ Supported
☐ Protected
☐ Happy
☐ Optimistic
☐ In Love
☐ Sad
☐ Angry
☐ Scared
☐ Unsupported
☐ Content

Today's Date:

I Feel:

☐ Supported
☐ Protected
☐ Happy
☐ Optimistic
☐ In Love
☐ Sad
☐ Angry
☐ Scared
☐ Unsupported
☐ Content

My Feelings and Thoughts

Today's Date:

I Feel:

- ☐ Supported
- ☐ Protected
- ☐ Happy
- ☐ Optimistic
- ☐ In Love
- ☐ Sad
- ☐ Angry
- ☐ Scared
- ☐ Unsupported
- ☐ Content

Today's Date:

I Feel:
☐ Supported
☐ Protected
☐ Happy
☐ Optimistic
☐ In Love
☐ Sad
☐ Angry
☐ Scared
☐ Unsupported
☐ Content

My Feelings and Thoughts

Today's Date:

Today's Date:

I Feel:

☐ Supported
☐ Protected
☐ Happy
☐ Optimistic
☐ In Love
☐ Sad
☐ Angry
☐ Scared
☐ Unsupported
☐ Content

My Feelings and Thoughts

Today's Date:

I Feel:

- ☐ Supported
- ☐ Protected
- ☐ Happy
- ☐ Optimistic
- ☐ In Love
- ☐ Sad
- ☐ Angry
- ☐ Scared
- ☐ Unsupported
- ☐ Content

My Feelings and Thoughts

Today's Date:

I Feel:
☐ Supported
☐ Protected
☐ Happy
☐ Optimistic
☐ In Love
☐ Sad
☐ Angry
☐ Scared
☐ Unsupported
☐ Content

Today's Date:

I Feel:

☐ Supported
☐ Protected
☐ Happy
☐ Optimistic
☐ In Love
☐ Sad
☐ Angry
☐ Scared
☐ Unsupported
☐ Content

Today's Date:

I Feel:

- ☐ Supported
- ☐ Protected
- ☐ Happy
- ☐ Optimistic
- ☐ In Love
- ☐ Sad
- ☐ Angry
- ☐ Scared
- ☐ Unsupported
- ☐ Content

My Feelings and Thoughts

Today's Date:

I Feel:

- ☐ Supported
- ☐ Protected
- ☐ Happy
- ☐ Optimistic
- ☐ In Love
- ☐ Sad
- ☐ Angry
- ☐ Scared
- ☐ Unsupported
- ☐ Content

My Feelings and Thoughts

Today's Date:

I Feel:

- ☐ Supported
- ☐ Protected
- ☐ Happy
- ☐ Optimistic
- ☐ In Love
- ☐ Sad
- ☐ Angry
- ☐ Scared
- ☐ Unsupported
- ☐ Content

My Feelings and Thoughts

Today's Date:

Today's Date:

<table>
<tr><td>

I Feel:

☐ Supported
☐ Protected
☐ Happy
☐ Optimistic
☐ In Love
☐ Sad
☐ Angry
☐ Scared
☐ Unsupported
☐ Content

</td></tr>
</table>

My Feelings and Thoughts

Today's Date:

I Feel:

- ☐ Supported
- ☐ Protected
- ☐ Happy
- ☐ Optimistic
- ☐ In Love
- ☐ Sad
- ☐ Angry
- ☐ Scared
- ☐ Unsupported
- ☐ Content

My Feelings and Thoughts

Today's Date:

I Feel:

- ☐ Supported
- ☐ Protected
- ☐ Happy
- ☐ Optimistic
- ☐ In Love
- ☐ Sad
- ☐ Angry
- ☐ Scared
- ☐ Unsupported
- ☐ Content

My Feelings and Thoughts

Today's Date:

I Feel:

- ☐ Supported
- ☐ Protected
- ☐ Happy
- ☐ Optimistic
- ☐ In Love
- ☐ Sad
- ☐ Angry
- ☐ Scared
- ☐ Unsupported
- ☐ Content

Today's Date:

I Feel:

☐ Supported
☐ Protected
☐ Happy
☐ Optimistic
☐ In Love
☐ Sad
☐ Angry
☐ Scared
☐ Unsupported
☐ Content

My Feelings and Thoughts

Today's Date:

I Feel:

- ☐ Supported
- ☐ Protected
- ☐ Happy
- ☐ Optimistic
- ☐ In Love
- ☐ Sad
- ☐ Angry
- ☐ Scared
- ☐ Unsupported
- ☐ Content

My Feelings and Thoughts

Today's Date:

I Feel:
☐ Supported
☐ Protected
☐ Happy
☐ Optimistic
☐ In Love
☐ Sad
☐ Angry
☐ Scared
☐ Unsupported
☐ Content

My Feelings and Thoughts

Today's Date:

My Feelings and Thoughts

Today's Date:

I Feel:

- ☐ Supported
- ☐ Protected
- ☐ Happy
- ☐ Optimistic
- ☐ In Love
- ☐ Sad
- ☐ Angry
- ☐ Scared
- ☐ Unsupported
- ☐ Content

My Feelings and Thoughts

Today's Date:

I Feel:

- ☐ Supported
- ☐ Protected
- ☐ Happy
- ☐ Optimistic
- ☐ In Love
- ☐ Sad
- ☐ Angry
- ☐ Scared
- ☐ Unsupported
- ☐ Content

My Feelings and Thoughts

Today's Date:

I Feel:

- ☐ Supported
- ☐ Protected
- ☐ Happy
- ☐ Optimistic
- ☐ In Love
- ☐ Sad
- ☐ Angry
- ☐ Scared
- ☐ Unsupported
- ☐ Content

My Feelings and Thoughts

Today's Date:

I Feel:

- ☐ Supported
- ☐ Protected
- ☐ Happy
- ☐ Optimistic
- ☐ In Love
- ☐ Sad
- ☐ Angry
- ☐ Scared
- ☐ Unsupported
- ☐ Content

Today's Date:

I Feel:
☐ Supported
☐ Protected
☐ Happy
☐ Optimistic
☐ In Love
☐ Sad
☐ Angry
☐ Scared
☐ Unsupported
☐ Content

Today's Date:

I Feel:

☐ Supported
☐ Protected
☐ Happy
☐ Optimistic
☐ In Love
☐ Sad
☐ Angry
☐ Scared
☐ Unsupported
☐ Content

Today's Date:

My Feelings and Thoughts

Today's Date:

I Feel:

- ☐ Supported
- ☐ Protected
- ☐ Happy
- ☐ Optimistic
- ☐ In Love
- ☐ Sad
- ☐ Angry
- ☐ Scared
- ☐ Unsupported
- ☐ Content

My Feelings and Thoughts

Today's Date:

I Feel:

- ☐ Supported
- ☐ Protected
- ☐ Happy
- ☐ Optimistic
- ☐ In Love
- ☐ Sad
- ☐ Angry
- ☐ Scared
- ☐ Unsupported
- ☐ Content

My Feelings and Thoughts

Today's Date:

I Feel:

☐ Supported
☐ Protected
☐ Happy
☐ Optimistic
☐ In Love
☐ Sad
☐ Angry
☐ Scared
☐ Unsupported
☐ Content

Today's Date:

I Feel:

- ☐ Supported
- ☐ Protected
- ☐ Happy
- ☐ Optimistic
- ☐ In Love
- ☐ Sad
- ☐ Angry
- ☐ Scared
- ☐ Unsupported
- ☐ Content

My Feelings and Thoughts

Today's Date:

I Feel:
☐ Supported
☐ Protected
☐ Happy
☐ Optimistic
☐ In Love
☐ Sad
☐ Angry
☐ Scared
☐ Unsupported
☐ Content

My Feelings and Thoughts

Today's Date:

	I Feel:
	☐ Supported
	☐ Protected
	☐ Happy
	☐ Optimistic
	☐ In Love
	☐ Sad
	☐ Angry
	☐ Scared
	☐ Unsupported
	☐ Content

My Feelings and Thoughts

Today's Date:

I Feel:

- ☐ Supported
- ☐ Protected
- ☐ Happy
- ☐ Optimistic
- ☐ In Love
- ☐ Sad
- ☐ Angry
- ☐ Scared
- ☐ Unsupported
- ☐ Content

Today's Date:

I Feel:

- ☐ Supported
- ☐ Protected
- ☐ Happy
- ☐ Optimistic
- ☐ In Love
- ☐ Sad
- ☐ Angry
- ☐ Scared
- ☐ Unsupported
- ☐ Content

My Feelings and Thoughts

Today's Date:

I Feel:
☐ Supported
☐ Protected
☐ Happy
☐ Optimistic
☐ In Love
☐ Sad
☐ Angry
☐ Scared
☐ Unsupported
☐ Content

My Feelings and Thoughts

Today's Date:

I Feel:

- ☐ Supported
- ☐ Protected
- ☐ Happy
- ☐ Optimistic
- ☐ In Love
- ☐ Sad
- ☐ Angry
- ☐ Scared
- ☐ Unsupported
- ☐ Content

Today's Date:

____

____

____

____

____

____

____

I Feel:
☐ Supported
☐ Protected
☐ Happy
☐ Optimistic
☐ In Love
☐ Sad
☐ Angry
☐ Scared
☐ Unsupported
☐ Content

My Feelings and Thoughts

Today's Date:

I Feel:
☐ Supported
☐ Protected
☐ Happy
☐ Optimistic
☐ In Love
☐ Sad
☐ Angry
☐ Scared
☐ Unsupported
☐ Content

My Feelings and Thoughts

Today's Date:

I Feel:

- ☐ Supported
- ☐ Protected
- ☐ Happy
- ☐ Optimistic
- ☐ In Love
- ☐ Sad
- ☐ Angry
- ☐ Scared
- ☐ Unsupported
- ☐ Content

My Feelings and Thoughts

Today's Date:

My Feelings and Thoughts

Today's Date:

I Feel:

- ☐ Supported
- ☐ Protected
- ☐ Happy
- ☐ Optimistic
- ☐ In Love
- ☐ Sad
- ☐ Angry
- ☐ Scared
- ☐ Unsupported
- ☐ Content

My Feelings and Thoughts

Today's Date:

____

I Feel:
☐ Supported
☐ Protected
☐ Happy
☐ Optimistic
☐ In Love
☐ Sad
☐ Angry
☐ Scared
☐ Unsupported
☐ Content

Today's Date:

I Feel:
☐ Supported
☐ Protected
☐ Happy
☐ Optimistic
☐ In Love
☐ Sad
☐ Angry
☐ Scared
☐ Unsupported
☐ Content

My Feelings and Thoughts

Today's Date:

My Feelings and Thoughts

Today's Date:

<table>
<tr><td>

I Feel:

- ☐ Supported
- ☐ Protected
- ☐ Happy
- ☐ Optimistic
- ☐ In Love
- ☐ Sad
- ☐ Angry
- ☐ Scared
- ☐ Unsupported
- ☐ Content

</td></tr>
</table>

My Feelings and Thoughts

Today's Date:

Today's Date:

I Feel:

☐ Supported
☐ Protected
☐ Happy
☐ Optimistic
☐ In Love
☐ Sad
☐ Angry
☐ Scared
☐ Unsupported
☐ Content

My Feelings and Thoughts

Today's Date:

I Feel:

- ☐ Supported
- ☐ Protected
- ☐ Happy
- ☐ Optimistic
- ☐ In Love
- ☐ Sad
- ☐ Angry
- ☐ Scared
- ☐ Unsupported
- ☐ Content

Today's Date:

My Feelings and Thoughts

Today's Date:

My Feelings and Thoughts

Today's Date:

I Feel:

- ☐ Supported
- ☐ Protected
- ☐ Happy
- ☐ Optimistic
- ☐ In Love
- ☐ Sad
- ☐ Angry
- ☐ Scared
- ☐ Unsupported
- ☐ Content

My Feelings and Thoughts

Today's Date:

My Feelings and Thoughts

Today's Date:

I Feel:

- ☐ Supported
- ☐ Protected
- ☐ Happy
- ☐ Optimistic
- ☐ In Love
- ☐ Sad
- ☐ Angry
- ☐ Scared
- ☐ Unsupported
- ☐ Content

Today's Date:

I Feel:
☐ Supported
☐ Protected
☐ Happy
☐ Optimistic
☐ In Love
☐ Sad
☐ Angry
☐ Scared
☐ Unsupported
☐ Content

Today's Date:

<table>
<tr><td>

____

____

____

____

____

</td><td>

I Feel:

☐ Supported
☐ Protected
☐ Happy
☐ Optimistic
☐ In Love
☐ Sad
☐ Angry
☐ Scared
☐ Unsupported
☐ Content

</td></tr>
</table>

My Feelings and Thoughts

Today's Date:

	I Feel:
	☐ Supported
	☐ Protected
	☐ Happy
	☐ Optimistic
	☐ In Love
	☐ Sad
	☐ Angry
	☐ Scared
	☐ Unsupported
	☐ Content

My Feelings and Thoughts

Today's Date:

I Feel:

- ☐ Supported
- ☐ Protected
- ☐ Happy
- ☐ Optimistic
- ☐ In Love
- ☐ Sad
- ☐ Angry
- ☐ Scared
- ☐ Unsupported
- ☐ Content

My Feelings and Thoughts

Today's Date:

Today's Date:

____

____

____

____

____

____

____

____

I Feel:

☐ Supported
☐ Protected
☐ Happy
☐ Optimistic
☐ In Love
☐ Sad
☐ Angry
☐ Scared
☐ Unsupported
☐ Content

____

____

____

____

____

____

____

____

____

____

____

____

____

____

____

My Feelings and Thoughts

Today's Date:

I Feel:

- ☐ Supported
- ☐ Protected
- ☐ Happy
- ☐ Optimistic
- ☐ In Love
- ☐ Sad
- ☐ Angry
- ☐ Scared
- ☐ Unsupported
- ☐ Content

Today's Date:

My Feelings and Thoughts

Today's Date:

I Feel:

☐ Supported
☐ Protected
☐ Happy
☐ Optimistic
☐ In Love
☐ Sad
☐ Angry
☐ Scared
☐ Unsupported
☐ Content

My Feelings and Thoughts

Today's Date:

I Feel:

- ☐ Supported
- ☐ Protected
- ☐ Happy
- ☐ Optimistic
- ☐ In Love
- ☐ Sad
- ☐ Angry
- ☐ Scared
- ☐ Unsupported
- ☐ Content

My Feelings and Thoughts

Today's Date:

I Feel:

☐ Supported
☐ Protected
☐ Happy
☐ Optimistic
☐ In Love
☐ Sad
☐ Angry
☐ Scared
☐ Unsupported
☐ Content

My Feelings and Thoughts

Today's Date:

I Feel:

- ☐ Supported
- ☐ Protected
- ☐ Happy
- ☐ Optimistic
- ☐ In Love
- ☐ Sad
- ☐ Angry
- ☐ Scared
- ☐ Unsupported
- ☐ Content

My Feelings and Thoughts

Today's Date:

I Feel:

☐ Supported
☐ Protected
☐ Happy
☐ Optimistic
☐ In Love
☐ Sad
☐ Angry
☐ Scared
☐ Unsupported
☐ Content

My Feelings and Thoughts

Today's Date:

I Feel:

- ☐ Supported
- ☐ Protected
- ☐ Happy
- ☐ Optimistic
- ☐ In Love
- ☐ Sad
- ☐ Angry
- ☐ Scared
- ☐ Unsupported
- ☐ Content

My Feelings and Thoughts

Today's Date:

I Feel:

- ☐ Supported
- ☐ Protected
- ☐ Happy
- ☐ Optimistic
- ☐ In Love
- ☐ Sad
- ☐ Angry
- ☐ Scared
- ☐ Unsupported
- ☐ Content

Today's Date:

I Feel:

☐ Supported
☐ Protected
☐ Happy
☐ Optimistic
☐ In Love
☐ Sad
☐ Angry
☐ Scared
☐ Unsupported
☐ Content

Today's Date:

____

____

____

____

____

____

____

I Feel:
☐ Supported
☐ Protected
☐ Happy
☐ Optimistic
☐ In Love
☐ Sad
☐ Angry
☐ Scared
☐ Unsupported
☐ Content

____

____

____

____

____

____

____

____

____

____

____

____

____

____

____

____

Today's Date:

I Feel:

☐ Supported
☐ Protected
☐ Happy
☐ Optimistic
☐ In Love
☐ Sad
☐ Angry
☐ Scared
☐ Unsupported
☐ Content

Today's Date:

I Feel:
☐ Supported
☐ Protected
☐ Happy
☐ Optimistic
☐ In Love
☐ Sad
☐ Angry
☐ Scared
☐ Unsupported
☐ Content

Today's Date:

I Feel:

- ☐ Supported
- ☐ Protected
- ☐ Happy
- ☐ Optimistic
- ☐ In Love
- ☐ Sad
- ☐ Angry
- ☐ Scared
- ☐ Unsupported
- ☐ Content

Today's Date:

I Feel:
☐ Supported
☐ Protected
☐ Happy
☐ Optimistic
☐ In Love
☐ Sad
☐ Angry
☐ Scared
☐ Unsupported
☐ Content

Today's Date:

I Feel:

☐ Supported
☐ Protected
☐ Happy
☐ Optimistic
☐ In Love
☐ Sad
☐ Angry
☐ Scared
☐ Unsupported
☐ Content

My Feelings and Thoughts

Today's Date:

I Feel:

- ☐ Supported
- ☐ Protected
- ☐ Happy
- ☐ Optimistic
- ☐ In Love
- ☐ Sad
- ☐ Angry
- ☐ Scared
- ☐ Unsupported
- ☐ Content

Today's Date:

Today's Date:

I Feel:
- ☐ Supported
- ☐ Protected
- ☐ Happy
- ☐ Optimistic
- ☐ In Love
- ☐ Sad
- ☐ Angry
- ☐ Scared
- ☐ Unsupported
- ☐ Content

My Feelings and Thoughts

Today's Date:

I Feel:

☐ Supported
☐ Protected
☐ Happy
☐ Optimistic
☐ In Love
☐ Sad
☐ Angry
☐ Scared
☐ Unsupported
☐ Content

Today's Date:

____

____

____

____

____

____

____

I Feel:
☐ Supported
☐ Protected
☐ Happy
☐ Optimistic
☐ In Love
☐ Sad
☐ Angry
☐ Scared
☐ Unsupported
☐ Content

____

____

____

____

____

____

____

____

____

____

____

____

____

____

My Feelings and Thoughts

Today's Date:

I Feel:

☐ Supported
☐ Protected
☐ Happy
☐ Optimistic
☐ In Love
☐ Sad
☐ Angry
☐ Scared
☐ Unsupported
☐ Content

My Feelings and Thoughts

Today's Date:

I Feel:

- ☐ Supported
- ☐ Protected
- ☐ Happy
- ☐ Optimistic
- ☐ In Love
- ☐ Sad
- ☐ Angry
- ☐ Scared
- ☐ Unsupported
- ☐ Content

Today's Date:

I Feel:

☐ Supported
☐ Protected
☐ Happy
☐ Optimistic
☐ In Love
☐ Sad
☐ Angry
☐ Scared
☐ Unsupported
☐ Content

Today's Date:

I Feel:

☐ Supported
☐ Protected
☐ Happy
☐ Optimistic
☐ In Love
☐ Sad
☐ Angry
☐ Scared
☐ Unsupported
☐ Content

My Feelings and Thoughts

Today's Date:

I Feel:

☐ Supported
☐ Protected
☐ Happy
☐ Optimistic
☐ In Love
☐ Sad
☐ Angry
☐ Scared
☐ Unsupported
☐ Content

Today's Date:

I Feel:

☐ Supported
☐ Protected
☐ Happy
☐ Optimistic
☐ In Love
☐ Sad
☐ Angry
☐ Scared
☐ Unsupported
☐ Content

My Feelings and Thoughts

Today's Date:

My Feelings and Thoughts

Today's Date:

I Feel:
☐ Supported
☐ Protected
☐ Happy
☐ Optimistic
☐ In Love
☐ Sad
☐ Angry
☐ Scared
☐ Unsupported
☐ Content

My Feelings and Thoughts

Today's Date:

I Feel:

- ☐ Supported
- ☐ Protected
- ☐ Happy
- ☐ Optimistic
- ☐ In Love
- ☐ Sad
- ☐ Angry
- ☐ Scared
- ☐ Unsupported
- ☐ Content

My Feelings and Thoughts

Today's Date:

I Feel:

- ☐ Supported
- ☐ Protected
- ☐ Happy
- ☐ Optimistic
- ☐ In Love
- ☐ Sad
- ☐ Angry
- ☐ Scared
- ☐ Unsupported
- ☐ Content

My Feelings and Thoughts

Today's Date:

Today's Date:

<table><tr><td>

</td><td>

I Feel:

- ☐ Supported
- ☐ Protected
- ☐ Happy
- ☐ Optimistic
- ☐ In Love
- ☐ Sad
- ☐ Angry
- ☐ Scared
- ☐ Unsupported
- ☐ Content

</td></tr></table>

My Feelings and Thoughts

Today's Date:

I Feel:

- ☐ Supported
- ☐ Protected
- ☐ Happy
- ☐ Optimistic
- ☐ In Love
- ☐ Sad
- ☐ Angry
- ☐ Scared
- ☐ Unsupported
- ☐ Content

Today's Date:

I Feel:
☐ Supported
☐ Protected
☐ Happy
☐ Optimistic
☐ In Love
☐ Sad
☐ Angry
☐ Scared
☐ Unsupported
☐ Content

My Feelings and Thoughts

Today's Date:

Kinyatta E. Gray is a Best-Selling Author, Travel Influencer and the CEO of FlightsInStilettos, LLC. Kinyatta is also the Chief Beach Towel Designer for the FlightsInStilettos Glam Girl Beach Towels.

Websites:

https://www.flightsinstilettos.com/

https://www.kinyattagray.com/

https://www.honoringmissbee.com/